WHAT MY HEART DESIRES

ANN M HAMPTON

What My Heart Desires
Written by Ann M. Hampton

ISBN -9780977116034

Published by Vaughanworks,
P.O. Box 44224
West Allis, Wisconsin, 53214,
vaughanworks@sbcglobal.net
1-877-829-6757

Biography

Ann Hampton, a loving devoted wife, mother and grandmother was born and raised in Milwaukee, Wisconsin. She now resides with her husband Robert, in Phoenix, Arizona.

At an early age, Ann wrote and sold songs to local groups. Each time she picked up a pen and paper, she found herself writing stories or poems. After running a successful business and a long career in the corporate world, on the advice of her husband, she decided to step out on faith and begin a professional writing career.

Her first book, What My Heart Desires, helps the reader understand the consequences they face when personal desires overtake reason.

Chapter 1

It is a cold, winter day. As I awaken, I see snow gently falling through the textured window. To the right of me is an unusual looking telephone. On the left side is a Chicago Newspaper laying on the table. The room itself is an eerie off-white. I ask myself what happened. Where am I? How did I get here? I try to run, but I feel myself wanting to cry because I cannot move. Just then there was a knock on the door and a man came in asking me how I was doing today. I saw him, but could not speak. He pulled up a chair, put on a pair of reading glasses and began to read to me from his black book. My mind was elsewhere, so I didn't understand exactly what he was saying.

While he continued to read, it all started to slowly come back to me, the love, betrayal, and lies. The more I watched him, the more I began to question myself and ask questions. How did I let my life get to this point and what could I have done differently to change the situation? My name is Tracy Moore and this is my story.

I grew up in Atlanta Georgia. My mother raised six of us as a single parent. I always wanted to be a medical doctor after my twin sister Trina took sick and died. We were so close and her death really broke my heart. I never did become a doctor, but I obtained my degree in nursing. I am one of those ladies that always ends up with the wrong man no matter what I do. I have been in and out of relationships, some were very abusive physically and mentally. I finally thought I had found the man of my dreams, but I walked in on him making love to another woman. I could not take it anymore and moved to Chicago on the advice of my cousin Brenda and her husband Marcus. I began to work for St Anne's Hospital in Chicago. Brenda and Marcus would always have get-togethers and introduce me to their friends. At one of their parties Brenda introduced me to a wonderful couple, Richard and Jackie Love.

Richard, a thirty five year old, clean-shaven, muscular man was always telling or playing jokes on people. Jackie was Ms. Know-it-all. You could not tell her anything because she was the kind of person who was always right about everything. I liked Jackie because she was never afraid to speak her mind. I became really close to them because among their other businesses, they ran a shelter for abused women. I would often provide food, clothing, medical care and advice to the women being a victim myself.

The years passed and it seemed Richard and Jackie were having problems and arguing more and more. She took things seriously, while Richard did not take things seriously enough. I don't know when it happened, but the more I worked with Richard at the shelter, the more we found out that we had a lot of things in common. He was so kind and kept me laughing.

It felt good to laugh because I have been hurt, sad, and disappointed so many times. When I laughed, it helped me forget my problems. I remember one time he called himself trying to tell a joke and he forgot the punch line. It was hilarious. He was a fun loving person, but he was also so sincere, kind and the gentlest man I had ever known.

One day after work my car broke down in the rain. I could not get a hold of either Brenda or Marcus. As faith would have it Jackie and Richard had one of their spats and he left the house to cool off. He happened to see me in the rain trying to call for help. He pulled over, tried to get my car started. When he couldn't, he called for a tow truck and waited in the car with me. I was thankful that this all took place on a Friday night because they had to keep my car for repairs overnight. Richard offered to drive me home and pick me up to get my car the next day.

He was such a gentleman, putting his jacket over me and offering to walk me to my door. He also made sure I was ok because I was wet and cold. I don't know if it was his kindness or the fact that I really enjoyed being around him that made me say yes when he asked to come in just for a moment. He said he wanted to talk with me.

I poured us both a glass of wine, turned on the television and one of my favorite movies Love Jones was on. It happened to be one of his favorites also. When we consumed the wine and watched the movie, I felt a warm, exciting feeling come over me. I think it was because of the way Richard looked at me. I was so confused and asked him to leave. When he got up from the couch, he rubbed against me. It had been a long time since I had been with a man. When he touched me, it turned both of us on. Soon, we began to kiss and make love passionately. We were so into each other that we both did not think about the consequences of our action and how it would affect Jackie. After that evening, Richard and I were together every chance we got. The affair had been going on for almost two years and no one had the slightest clue.

One day at a fundraiser for the organization, Jackie introduced me to a close friend, Troy Johnson. Troy was an executive for another chapter in their organization and had just moved to Chicago. Troy was a very handsome man with the most gorgeous eyes that I have ever seen and a smile that could light any room. He was well-built, like he worked out. He wore a brown v-neck sweater that hugged his chest nicely and dark brown pants to match. He looked as though he stepped out of vogue magazine.

I was so busy checking him out that I almost missed his conversation. He told me he was the CEO and owner of Johnson Brothers Group, an advertising agency that he owns with his three brothers, James, Mike, and Steve. Mike is part owner in the business, but hasn't done much work for the company. He was now ready to roll up his sleeve, take action, and get busy since they were opening their second office in Chicago. James was the face of the organization, promoting the agency to the public. Steve, on the other hand, has always been a hard worker for the firm, bringing new clients and running the daily activities. To my surprise, their corporate office happened to be in Atlanta, my home-town, but I never heard of them until we met.

Troy and I started to talk. I found out that he had been friends with Richard over ten years. He had not dated since his wife died two years ago. In talking to Troy I found out he was an individual that was very kind, deep, and passionate about his work. It was fun talking to him because we knew some of the same people and could laugh about events that happened in the past. As time passed we became friends. He was like an older brother to me.

One weekend, Richard told Jackie he had to go out of town on business when it really was a time for us to spend the weekend together at a resort in Florida. Troy was at the same resort to attend a meeting with a potential client of his. While we were at the restaurant, he saw us kissing at the dinner table. Later, he saw us romantically dancing at a club in the resort. He saw us leave together and take an elevator to our room. After that weekend, Troy acted funny around us and never mentioned what he saw until later on. It was a time when Troy and Richard had a disagreement about an issue. Troy brought it up and wanted to know what was going on? Richard was shocked and asked Troy not to mention it to Jackie because it would break her heart. Troy agreed.

The affair between Richard and I went on a few more years and I was beginning to feel sad and lonely, especially around the Holidays. I was alone and saw less and less of Richard. I didn't know if he was getting tired of me, if I was becoming tired of being the other woman in his life or if he was just taking me for granted.

Chapter 2

The next week Richard and Jackie obtained a huge grant for their organization and they celebrated with a party at their home. Richard started playing a love song on the piano. I watched Jackie sit at the piano beside him. She loved every moment. Some people danced and others gathered around the couple. When it was over, they gave each other a passionate kiss and everyone cheered, but it broke my heart. I felt like I was being used. I was so tired of that. I wanted to run over there and tell Jackie what a rat Richard is, but, I loved him and she is such a nice person. I didn't want to see her hurt.

I felt so dirty and confused that I couldn't stand it anymore. I felt like my heart was breaking especially after seeing them kiss like that. I decided to go outside so no one else could see me cry, but Richard did and asked Troy to keep Jackie busy while he talked to me. Troy did not like it, but he had been doing this for so awhile now and could not stop.

Richard came outside stood behind me.

"Did you like your song?"

"What do you mean by my song?" I replied.

"Don't you mean Jackie's song?"

"Honey, you know I wrote that song for you."

"Richard, aren't you taking a big chance coming out here to talk to me like this while Jackie is in the house."

"I suppose your right, but you still did not answer my question."

"Did you like your song?" he asked.

"Yes Richard. It was nice."

"You know how I feel about you. I love you so much and I want to be close to you."

I became irritated.

"You keep saying that, yet you won't divorce Jackie and I feel like you're keeping me around for your pleasure."

Before he could respond, Troy tapped on the window to let him know that Jackie was looking for him and was about to come outside, so he told me that we would finish this conversation later.

I went back inside for a few minutes and asked my friend Sharon to take me home. Sharon was having a great time and did not want to leave just yet. Troy overhearing the conversation volunteered to take me home.

After the usual hugs and good-bye's, Troy walked me to his car and he opened the door.

"You look like you could use a nice cup of coffee and some conversation," he stated.

"No thank you," I said with tears in my eyes. "I just want to go home."

At that point, Troy pulled me close to his body.

"Tracy, I cannot hold back my feelings any longer. You are not the only one that has been hurt by love. There is someone else who is suffering the agony of wanting to be with someone. I know someone else who would love to be held and loved, but could not or would not out of loyalty to a friend. I feel we really should talk."

"Troy, you sound like you are talking about yourself."

To my surprise he answered, "I am."

"Who is this woman you have wanted to be with?"

"I'm looking at her now," he said.

"It's me?"

"Tracy, I fell in love with you long ago. I did not say anything to you because I knew you were involved with Richard, but I cannot stand seeing the hurt in your eyes again. He does not deserve you. I know you feel you are his lady and I am his friend, but I can't stand the way he uses people for his personal desire. You deserve better than that. Can we go somewhere and talk?"

"Troy, I would like that. I know we have been close friends, but I never knew you felt that way."

Richard was peeping out the window and

became curious about what we were discussing. He even started to become a bit jealous because Troy was holding me a little too close.

Troy and I went to a romantic revolving restaurant in the Plaza Hotel. We were so high that we could see the gorgeous lights all around the city. Inside the restaurant was a piano bar and a water fountain surrounded by a variety of fresh flowers and plants. I did not even know a place like this existed, not that I have been dating anyone else. It was perfect and I felt so happy and content. He seized the opportunity to pour his heart out to me. I knew we had some things in common but I didn't realize how deep we were. I was so into Troy and did not give Richard a second thought. Was I so strung out on Richard, that I never considered Troy a potential boyfriend?

After a few drinks, coffee, dessert, and the most wonderful, fulfilling conversation, it was time to leave and go back to the real world. Several hours passed before we arrived back to my apartment. A strange feeling came over me. I asked myself was I feeling this way because I was lonely, really liked Troy, or just wanting to get even with Richard. Whatever the reason I had a wonderful time with Troy. I even gave him a kiss on the cheek before going in. Troy seemed happy because he finally was free to let me know how he felt.

My cell phone was off and when I checked it I noticed that Richard had called several times. It happened to be the night he decided to jump in his car to spy on me. Maybe he was just concerned. He would have to pull up just as I gave Troy a kiss on the cheek. He was about to explode when he saw that kiss, even though it was on the cheek. He thought that I was his woman and Troy had no business being with me. He did not confront Troy but pounded on my door after Troy pulled off.

I opened the door and was surprised to find Richard standing there looking like a kid that had lost his lunch money.

"Richard, what are you doing here?" I asked.

"I called to make sure you made it home all right and when there was no answer, I became worried and came right over."

"Oh. I see. I wish you hadn't gone through all that trouble. As you can see, I'm fine and in one piece."

"So did Troy enjoy his little kiss?" "Richard! You are unbelievable. What is the matter with you? Have you stooped to spying on me now? Are you trying to take my freedom away? Or is it that you don't trust me. Do you feel threatened because someone else paid a little attention to me? Troy is a friend and he knows how hurt I was and all he did was try to comfort me. There is nothing going on between us. Sure, I gave him a kiss to thank him for listening to my problems. And you felt you could not come to me with your problems?"

I took a deep breath.

"Richard, you have Jackie to keep you warm at night. Who do I have? Besides, when I do want to speak with you I can't do it because you are with Jackie. I have to sneak around like I am some sort of closet lover. Night after night I fall asleep alone, wishing you were there to keep me warm and that you will be there in the morning, but when I wake, it is to a lonely apartment."

Richard replied, "Tracy, you know the situation. If I could I would love to be here with you when you wake up rather than leaving in the middle of the night."

"Yes, I understand Richard."

I walked up to him so close that I could feel his heart beat. I asked him if he would stay with me a little while because I really needed to be with him. I wasn't ready for his response.

"Baby, I would love to but I can't. I must get back home before I'm missed, but I'll see you tomorrow."

I really wanted to tell him not to bother, but I accepted his quick kiss before leaving. Before he got fully out of the door, I began to have mixed feelings because I didn't tell the truth about myself and Troy. I don't know why, but I just could not bring myself to do it.

Richard and Troy had been friends a long time.

Troy hated himself for letting Richard talk him into helping him cover up this extramarital affair. Hiding this affair from Jackie was just one more thing that weighed heavy on his shoulders. Richard always claimed that he cared for Jackie but was not in love with her. He only married her because she was pregnant. He wanted to do right. She lost the baby and he stayed with her because he felt sorry about what happened.

She had a rough life and he was not ready to hurt her even if it means that he was not totally happy himself. I was sick of the deception.

I told myself I didn't want to spend the rest of my life being the other woman. Many times I wanted to pull away from Richard, but he was kind to me, satisfied me sexually, and was everything a woman could want in a man, except he was married. My thoughts immediately switched to Troy and the conversation we had at the restaurant. I wished we could duplicate that moment. All the meetings, parties, and trips we took as a group and he never let me know how he felt until that evening.

It was the end of October and for the next several weeks life went on almost as usual. The only difference was that Troy had now been calling me. He often asked me out on dates. I always refused because I was still involved with Richard.

Holidays were always a special time for me. This Thanksgiving was going to be especially nice because Richard is going to pretend to be out of town on business the day after Thanksgiving and I am going to meet him in California where we will spend the entire weekend together. I simply cannot wait.

As usual, things did not work out as we had planned. Richard and Jackie supposedly had family come in for the Holidays and it was his sister's birthday. They planned a semi-formal birthday party for her that Saturday at a popular resort. For the life of me I do not understand how they could pull this off at the last moment, but our plans had to be put on hold. They wanted everyone to attend and at first I refused but I had to see Richard and make him pay for his lying to me. I wanted him to look at me with such desire that he had to have me I had my hair done. After applying my makeup, I found the sexiest dress in my closet. It was a strapless red satin dress that hugged my body nicely with purse and shoes to match. I was the bell of the ball. Troy had asked me to attend the party with him as his date. I refused because I felt I was Richard's woman and I did not want to be unfaithful to him, though he was being unfaithful to his own wife.

At the party, everything started pretty much as normal. Richard, Jackie and the rest of the couples were together and I came with my friend Dee. A half hour later to my surprise Troy came in but not with his brother as usual, but a light skinned slender woman with reddish-brown hair and a stunning blue sequenced dressed. She looked like a fashion model. Richard was happy to see him with someone else but I was a little upset and it showed on my face as he was introducing her to me and some of his friends.

I looked around the room and saw Richard with Jackie, Troy with his date, and all the other couples and I began to feel really lonely. How stupid was I to show up at this party without a date. Suddenly, Richard approached me and I was so happy.

"Would you like to dance?"

"I'd love to, Richard."

I finally had a chance to be in the arms of my loved one. While we danced, he explained to me how sorry he was that we could not get together this weekend and promised me that we will get away the next weekend. The dance did not last too long as Jackie broke it up because she had something for him to do. That made me pretty angry. How dare she interrupt our dance? Then I realized that she is his wife.

I sat at one of the empty tables and started to drink. As I looked around the room there was Richard having fun with Jackie and Troy with his date. I thought to myself, what kind of desperate woman am I. Richard did not even tell me how good I look. The negative thoughts poured in. I continued to drink until I did not care about anyone or anything. I was beginning to hate all men because all they wanted was to use me.

I felt like someone had pulled the life out of me

and I lost everything and everyone. Just then some guy asked me to dance and I agreed so I could show off and shine. I wanted to show them that I was a desirable woman, so I started to bump and grind as they played Quincy Jones' Juke Joint. I was having fun and did not realize that I was turning this guy on. Troy did not like it, but Richard thought it was cute at first until I started rubbing on the guy.

Richard started to get a little upset because he did not like the way things were going on the dance floor. When the dance was over, I stumbled to the bar. Richard grabbed me.

"What is going on?" he asked.

"You are acting like a slut. I thought you were a classy woman." I slapped his face and left the bar with my drink. I found the guy I was dancing with and started to dance with him again. In the middle of the dance I began to feel sick and wanted to sit down, but the guy would not let me. He was pretty drunk himself and kept pulling and harassing me.

Just then Troy made his excuses to his date and stepped in to put an end to it. He told him, "Hey man, the lady has had enough." All Troy had to do was look at the guy and he threw up his hands and walked away. Troy was upset with me. He felt sorry for me and could tell I was hurting and not acting like myself. He walked me to the bathroom and after I threw up, I felt a little better. I am not a drinker. The most I ever have is a glass of wine and I was drinking hard liquor.

Troy told Jack the bartender to bring a pot of coffee on the patio ASAP. Once outside he managed to sit me down at the table and began to rub my face as he talked softly to me. He did not have an opportunity to get much of the conversation started because his date that was looking for him came outside and asked him what was going on. Richard and Jackie also came out on the patio. Troy left Tracy with Richard and Jackie as he explained to his date.

"Tracy is a close friend and she is ill. She has had a little too much to drink and I am making sure no one takes advantage of her."

"Well Troy, she snapped, I don't see how that is of any concern to you. She is a grown woman."

"Didn't I just explain that she is my friend? She needs help and I don't do my friends like that."

"Well look I am tired and ready to go home. Someone else can take care of her."

"Look, I am not going to leave her like this. Can't you wait just a few minutes?"

"No Troy, I want to leave now! "

"Don't you raise your voice at me! If you have to be that selfish and can't wait a minute, I'll call you a cab."

"Don't bother," she replied. "I'll get my own cab and you can forget about calling me or spending any time with me tonight."

She stormed back into the room where the other party guests were.

When Troy returned, Richard and Jackie were helping me drink coffee and talking to me because I was falling asleep.

I remember Troy looked angry when he returned. He told Richard and Jackie that he would see that I got home. Richard did not want to go but had to so Jackie would not get suspicious. I asked him why he was so angry with me. He explained that he was not angry just frustrated.

"Tracy I cannot understand what kind of hold Richard has on you to make you act this way."
I replied, "What makes you think that this has anything to do with Richard?"
Troy was puzzled.
"I am going to take you home."

Troy did not say very much to me in the car. It was a long ride home and I was becoming depressed. When we arrived at my apartment, he told me he would like to have dinner with me tomorrow night around 6:00 p.m. I agreed.

Chapter 3

The next evening as I prepared to go out with him for dinner I could not help but question myself. Why do I always choose the wrong men to get involved with? Why am I always leaving myself open to be hurt or rejected? The thought of losing Richard was bad enough, but I could have had a chance with Troy. I pushed him out of my life before we even got started.

Why did I even agree to go out with him tonight especially after I made a fool out of myself and embarrassed everyone? How can I face people again? I continued to torture myself with these negative thoughts and for no reason began to cry and break things. Half dressed, I poured myself a drink. Just then there was a knock on the door. It could not be Troy as it is only 5:00 p.m. To my surprise, it was Troy. He handed me a vase filled with a dozen long stem red roses. I was totally floored and held the door open for him as he brought in a duffle bag and several boxes.

"Troy, what's all this and what are you doing here?"

"What's the matter? You're not happy to see me?" Troy replied.

"Yes I'm very happy. You just caught me by surprise. The roses are beautiful but I look like a mess."

Troy immediately pulled me close to him.

"You always have and always will look beautiful to me. You evidently thought that I was being kind when I told you that I was in love with you but I am serious. Before this day is over, you are going to see how serious I am. I love you more than life itself and I don't care about Richard or anyone else. Today I'm going to finally feel what it's like to hold, be with, and make love with the woman I always loved."

He glanced around the room.

"Well there's no need for me to ask what you have been up to."

I was so embarrassed. Troy asked me to do him a favor.

"I want you to put on your sexiest gown and relax. I am going to prepare dinner for us and I don't want you to worry about a thing. Don't even worry about the house. Just leave everything to me."

I was overwhelmed, but did just as he asked. I could not believe that anyone would go to this extent to please me. Troy is such a wonderful, loving, caring man. I can feel his strength. After a wonderful romantic dinner, we retired to the couch to relax and watch a little TV. It felt so good being in his arms.

As we watched the movie, Troy began to kiss me on my lips.

"I know that Richard hurt you badly and I know he cares about you and you for him, although I wished you didn't, but he cannot love you the way I can. I want you to put Richard out of your mind at least for this evening. Besides, I could have told Jackie what was going on, but I wanted to protect you more than I wanted to protect him."

He moved closer to me.

"Tracy, I have been waiting a long time to be with you. Do you know how painful it was for me watching you with Richard when Jackie was not around? I wished it was me holding you, but not being able to let you know how I felt. Well, from this day on you are the only one that matters in my life."

I could not believe what I was hearing. I stood and walked to the other side of the room.

"Troy, this may surprise you, but I was more hurt at seeing you with that other woman. For some reason I wanted to be close to you. I felt I had lost you. I didn't realize how much I really cared for you until then."

Troy was so happy to hear those words that he grabbed me and pulled me close to his body.

"Tracy, I want you so badly, but I can't make love to you unless Richard is out of your system. I want you to be with me totally body, soul and mind. I don't want Richard to ever touch you again. Do you care enough for me to commit to me?"

I was so happy; I did not say a word I just started to undress. Troy was so happy. Finally, his dream came true.

Making love to Troy was incredible. The warmth of his body next to mine was pure ecstasy. We both knew that after this, there would be a fight against Richard but neither of us cared at the time. Richard had Jackie and now I have someone I can call my own. No more being alone or lonely nights. Jackie had Richard and I have Troy.

When Jackie and Richard arrived back at their home, she mentioned to him how nice it was for Troy to take care of me. I wished they could get together because they were made for each other. A chill suddenly came over Richard and he started to wonder if Troy was with me. After all, he was pretty cozy with her at the party. He called but there was no answer at Troy's house. His heart skipped a beat as he called me. I was still half sleep in Troy's arms when I answered the phone, but hearing Richard's voice quickly awakened me.

"Hello?"
"Hello beautiful. How are you doing?"
"Richard?"
"Who did you think it was? Were you asleep?"
"Yes, I was."
"Good. I'm on my way over there."

"What? "

I hopped out of the bed.

"You heard me, I will be there shortly."

Troy sat up with a puzzled look on his face.

"I don't think that that is a good idea."

"Why? You never thought it was a bad idea before. What's going on? Are you alone or do you have company?"

"Richard, why are you putting me through the third degree like this? You think you can just pop over anytime you want without regard to my privacy or what I am doing or might have planned."

"Sweetheart, I don't like the tone of your voice."

"Look Richard, it's late, I'm tired, and I've made other plans. I don't think it is a good idea for you to come over here."

"I'll be over there in ten minutes and you had better be alone because I don't want anyone messing around with my woman."

Before I could get another word out, he hung up the phone. I felt I was in a bad situation and became frantic. I started running around the house trying to clean up, find something decent to put on. I totally forgot about Troy and did not say a word to him. I did not want Richard to find me like that. I began to mumble to myself, he can't treat me like this; he can't do this to me. Who does he think he is anyway?

Troy asked, "What are you doing?"

"He's on his way over here now. "Who's on their

way over here?" he asked, knowing I was talking about Richard.

"Tell me something. Why didn't you give me the phone or tell him that I was here. Why are you trying to get the house in order for him? You belong to me now and he is just going to have to learn to live with that. We are together and we are going to face him together, unless you are planning on kicking me out."

"I'm really sorry Troy. I guess I just did not expect to have to confront him so soon with this. We've been together such a long time and I guess it's not as easy as I thought it was going to be to end the relationship."

"What are you trying to say? You don't care about me any longer?"

That's not it. I'm just saying I really don't want to hurt Richard. We have been together a long time."

"What do you mean hurt Richard? What about hurting me? What about my feelings and how long I've waited for you. You mean nothing to him but the other woman on the side."

Troy was becoming upset. Just then, the doorbell rang.

No one had to say a thing because the look on Richard's face said it all when I opened the door. Here was Troy, his best friend standing with a smug look on his face with nothing on but his underpants and me looking guilty. I think Troy intentionally did not put anything on.

"You low down dirty, back-stabbing son of a bitch."

Richard swung at Troy's face. That was it, the fight was on. They began to struggle and knock over anything that got in their way. They even knocked me down. I finally threw a vase at the wall and the two of them stopped.

"You two are acting like a couple of dogs fighting over a piece of meat. You come in here, wreck my apartment, and throw me against the wall without concern for my safety or my neighbors."

Richard grabbed me by the arm and started to force me into the bedroom saying, "I want to talk to you now!"

Troy was right behind him, trying to break the hold.

"What's the matter with you pulling on her like that? Anything you have to say you can say to us."

I knew I had to take control, so I walked toward Troy.

"Sweetheart, do you trust me?"

"Yes I trust you, but I don't trust him."

"Please let me talk to him alone just for a minute."

"Then talk," said a very unhappy Troy.

We went into the bedroom and a very hurt, confused Richard began to try to make sense of what he just witnessed.

"I don't understand you Tracy. I turn my back and you sleep with my boy."

"First of all, you don't know if I slept with him or not. For all you know I could have been sewing a button on his shirt or just needed someone to talk to. Besides, you're sleeping with Jackie."

"Jackie is my wife! I thought you were my lady and that you loved me."

Troy went out on the patio when he heard me say, "I do love you Richard." What he did not hear was the rest of the conversation.

"I love you as a companion, a friend, a one time lover, but I'm in love with Troy."

I don't know how, why or when it happened, it just happened and I could do nothing to stop it, nor did I want to. He has always been there for me. I just didn't know it until tonight.

"You're not making any sense," he replied. What in the hell do you mean a one time lover?"

"Richard, I'm tired of being a third wheel and your sex partner. You are never going to leave Jackie, we both know this. I need to feel as if I'm number one in my man's life and you can't give me that."

Troy decided to come back in to see if we were still talking and overheard pieces of the conversation. I was speaking softly, but Richard was loud.

"Baby, I love you so much and I don't want to lose you. If I divorce Jackie, would you stop this nonsense with Troy and come back to me where you belong?"

I just shook my head. Richard grabbed me and began to kiss me with a lot of passion from my lips down to my neck. I had to force myself and pull away when he made it to my breast. He was trying to seduce me into making love to him while Troy was in the other room.

"Richard, you love Jackie and you know you will never leave her. "

"Don't tell me what I will or will not do, just answer the question. If I divorce Jackie, will you leave Troy?"

"I'm sorry Richard; I can't make you a promise like that."

He tried again and held me even closer this time.

"Baby, you are a part of me. I will never let you go."

"Richard, I am sorry, but my place is now with Troy."

Richard walked out of the bedroom holding my hand and quickly glanced at Troy. He was leaning against the counter, still in his shorts, and drinking a bottle of beer. He moved toward the door.

"Remember what I said. I'll be back for you."

After Richard left, a very hurt and confused Troy went back out to the patio without saying a word and started staring straight ahead at the courtyard. I wanted to confront him and began to speak. He looked up at me and continued to drink without saying a word.

"Are you just going to sit there and ignore me?" He didn't speak. I was so mad I began to scream. "What the hell are you so mad about?" He finally replied. "It didn't take much, did it?" "What are you talking about?" "You know what I mean. I thought you were tougher than that. I thought we had something special going on and that you were in love with me, but it's Richard. It's always been and always will be Richard."

"I guess you are just another one of his trophies and I hope you will be really happy together after he divorces Jackie. I don't know how the bastard does it. He has a wife and a woman on the side and does not show respect for either one. I heard you tell him you loved him. You know, I use to have respect for you but now I can see why he doesn't respect you because you don't respect yourself."

After that I became mad, hurt, and angry all at the same time and slapped the hell out of him.

"How dare you talk to me that way? Who do you think you are? You come waltzing in here, pretending that you love, trust, and care about me and now that you made love to me you treat me like dirt. Maybe that's all you really wanted or maybe I wasn't good enough for you. Sure, I told Richard I loved him as a friend, but I was in love with you and there was no chance of us getting back together. You just can't turn love on and off like a faucet. Just because I still have some feelings for him, does not mean that I would disrespect you by sleeping with him. I told him that it did not matter what he does, I would never leave you, but I see I am fooling myself. You men are all the same. Just get out of my house and my life."

I ran to my bedroom and Troy feeling really bad ran after me. I was hurt and crying. He tried to hold me down and pressed harder on me. I began to fight him more, yelling,

"I thought you were different, but you're like the rest."

He was finally able to calm me and held me tightly on the bed. He had tears in his eyes.

"Baby, I'm a jealous fool. Please forgive me. I love you so much and I thought I was going to lose you and lost it. I would rather have someone rip out my tongue before I ever talk to you that way again."

He began to speak to me in his sweet soft sexy voice, sweetheart I am truly sorry for what I said and I need you. I began to relax and melt in his arms when he began to kiss my face, neck, shoulders and breast.

"I don't give a dam about Richard. He can't love you the way I can. Say you'll forgive me and I promise

I will never do or say anything to hurt you again. With tears in my eyes, I finally gave in and told him that I accepted his apology."

Chapter 4

After we made up, we decided to go for a drive to the lake to get some fresh air. It was so beautiful and peaceful watching the lights flicker on the water. We sat on the rocks and watched the water splash on our legs. We talked about our future plans and what we would like to accomplish. We had so much in common. I could tell the way Troy looked at me that he was not sure if I had truly forgiven him and I liked it that way.

I like to keep him guessing. In order to feel me out more, he asked me over to his place. It was getting a little chilly by the lake and he wanted to be in a different environment. When we arrived at his apartment, he built a fire in the fireplace and we sat on the carpet drinking champagne and watching the fire from the fireplace flicker off our bodies in the dark. He held me tight in his arms as though I was going to run away.

Richard, on the other hand was not having a good evening. He was angry with the thought of Troy sleeping with me and he began to fight with Jackie. At one point during the argument, he slipped and called

Jackie, Tracy.

"Tracy?" she replied. What the hell is going on here? Why are you calling me Tracy? Are you having an affair with that skinny bitch or something? Why is she on your mind?"

He knew he had blown it so he had to come up with a lie.

"I'm sorry honey, I was just thinking about Troy and Tracy and how much trouble she is in."

"What kind of trouble?"

"You must promise me that what I tell you will never leave this room. You can't share this with anyone."

"I promise," she replied.

"Troy is in big financial trouble with his business and has been involved in embezzlement. He is planning on romancing and marrying Tracy to get a hold of some big money she has. When his business takes off again, he plans on eliminating her and he wants me to help him with it."

"What? You mean he is going to kill her?"

I don't know what is going on. I tried to tell her she should take it slow with him but they really laid into me about it and now neither one will talk to me."

"Oh Richard, that's terrible."

"I know sweetheart."

"I'm sorry I accused you of being unfaithful and calling Tracy a bitch." I was just upset. Richard hugged her, with a smug smile on his face. He was the champion of all champions. Who else could lie on the spur of a moment? Now his wife is talking about helping him break up the relationship between his best friend and mistress.

She doesn't even know she is doing him the favor. Once they break them up, he can again reclaim her as his woman, because he felt in his heart he could not get enough of her.

The story he told was very convincing because Jackie knew that Troy's business was very important and he had been in financial trouble before. She knew that he would do anything to save his company from financial ruins. What she did not know was that his business was sound and growing stronger financially everyday.

The next few weeks following the incident, Richard kept calling me like we were still involved with each other. He not only came to my apartment several times, but my job causing problems. I kept Troy informed of everything. I thought Troy was going to become very angry but instead the conversation took another direction.

"Tracy, how is work? Are you happy doing what you are doing?"

"Well Troy, I used to be happy being a nurse and I still enjoy helping people, but things are not the same. The long hours are starting to get to me and I'm feeling burned out. I thought about changing gears and working for myself, but I don't know what else to do."

"I'm glad you said that because I would like for you to come in business with me"

"Troy, you have to be joking. I don't know anything about advertising."

"That is the beauty of it, I need someone by my side that I love and can trust to keep the business going. I will teach you everything and I promise you that you will be well paid."

"Troy I really love you and I don't want to ruin what we have going, but how is that going to work? Besides what would your employees say?"

"I don't care about what they think. Why don't you give it a try?"

"You mean you want me to just give up nursing after all this time?"

"Okay, hear me out. Why don't you start out as a personal assistant to me and health expert for our employees? You know we have several offices and it will do the employees good to learn how to take better care of themselves and increase productivity. You can talk to them about health and nutrition while you learn the business."

I was hesitant and scared, but the offer did appear good to me. If it did not work out, I could always go back to nursing. Every concern I had, Troy had the right answer until I finally accepted his offer. This could be so much fun, setting my hours and doing my thing. "

"Okay, how much am I going to be paid?"

"I will start you out at 15% more than you are making as a nurse and you have to move in with me."

"Troy, if I am going to do this, I must insist on keeping my own apartment."

"Ok, well let's move you into another apartment at least for now."

Troy kept his word. He provided me with my own office, recommended and paid for some online courses and started to teach me the business.

It's funny. Although I was busier, I was happier because I didn't have the pressure on me and I wasn't tied down to the office. Troy helped me to find a beautiful two bedroom condo. It was fantastic with an Oceanside view and in walking distance of a lot of shops and restaurants. Like any office environment there was some jealously, especially since they felt I was sleeping with the boss. There was a lot of gossip about where I came from and how I got an office. A couple of employees did not care for me and would do anything they could to sabotage me.

I tried my best to be friendly to everyone. I would bring treats and laugh at their not so funny jokes. I did manage to turn a few of them around.

Troy increased my responsibilities and had me to start contacting potential clients for him. His current office assistant Joanne did not like that because she felt that I was stepping into her territory. There was plenty for each of us to do. Troy gave me plenty of freedom to come and go as I pleased. I did not have to punch a clock. Sometimes, I would go to a nearby restaurant for lunch to relax and do some reading. This was my private quiet time to get away from the hustle of the office environment.

On one afternoon, I went to one of my favorite restaurants and I brought some paperwork with me. I was going to have a meeting with the staff and I wanted to make sure my thoughts were together. I was not paying much attention to what was going on around me. I happened to look up and saw Richard standing over me.

"How long have you been there?" I asked"
"I miss you Tracy."
I tried to grab my stuff and leave but he cornered me.
"Are you afraid of me or do you just hate me that much that you can't stand to give me a few minutes of your time."
I felt bad and sat down. Richard sat down next to me.

"I don't hate you Richard," I replied. "I just don't think it is a good idea for us to be seen alone together, especially since I am dating Troy."
"Why are you doing this to me? Did I treat you so badly that you have to run to my friend?"
"Richard, why can't you just be happy for me?

You have Jackie and you want to keep me on the side. I can't live like that anymore."

He began to rub my thigh under the table.

"I miss you so much. I need you and I want you back. A part of me is missing."

I felt myself becoming excited and not only did he look and smell good, but it felt good having him touch me like that again. I felt myself falling into a trap. I had to get away before I do something foolish, something I would regret. I threw my things in the briefcase and tried to leave but he would not let me out. I told him that if he did not move, I was going to scream. He finally moved and I headed straight for the door. Richard, feeling the vibe, ran after me. He would not let me get into my car.

He pulled me close to his body and whispered in my ear.

"I am going to ask Jackie for a divorce. I can't live without you any longer. When she is out of the picture, I am coming back for you."

"Richard I don't know how many times I have to tell you this, but I belong to Troy now."

"Well, I don't care what you say you belong to me and I will never let you go. We are one mind, body, and soul. I will never let you go. You are going to come to your senses and drop this nonsense with Troy. You know you don't want him you are just using him to get back at me because you feel somehow I hurt you. I know you moved out of your apartment but if you think you are going to get away from me you are crazy."

With that he tried to kiss me and I again became excited and did not want to pull away. I had to force myself to do so.

"I love you and I will never leave you and I will try every trick I can think of to destroy Troy and his business. He will not have anything to offer you when I am through with him."

That statement brought me down to earth. I broke away from him and jumped into the car. While all this was going on, two co-workers named Marcy and Jennifer saw the whole thing and could not wait to get back to the office to break the news to Troy.

I did not come back to the office right away. I drove to a park and cried. I was trying to figure out my emotions. I did love Troy but a part of me will always belong to Richard. Troy was the best thing that ever happened to me. He treated me like a queen, but I liked the way Richard felt next to me.

Back at the office a happy Marcy could not wait to tell Troy what she had seen. She had been crazy about Troy for sometime and he never showed her any interest. She poured out her guts and inflated the story even more. He figured out it was Richard from the description. He did not let Marcy know he was upset and told her to never bring gossip to him about the personal affairs of another employee. If she did, she can pack up and find another job.

When Marcy left his office, Troy became furious. He tried to work, but the thought of me once again in Richard's arms sent chills down his spine.

He threw the papers he was working on to the side and placed his head in his hands.

"What have I gotten myself into?" he thought. "Maybe I should hire a private investigator to follow her or get her a bodyguard."

While he considered his next move, I knocked on the door. I burst in, pretty upset.

"Troy, we have to talk."

Troy was not sure of what I was going to say and he was praying that I was not planning on going back to Richard. He slowly came from behind the desk and sat on the corner of it waiting to hear the bad news. I told him everything that had happened, including the threats.

"I love you Troy and I don't want to keep anything from you. I just didn't know what to do. I was so scared. A relieved Troy took her into his arms and told her not to worry.

"He will never bother you again."

Chapter 5

Troy and Richard belonged to the same health club owned by Dave, who was a mutual friend. It was early Saturday morning when Troy walked into the health club. He strolled past the weights and saw Richard riding on one of the bikes. He put a towel around his neck. Without saying a word, he jumped on and started riding the bike next to him. Richard stopped riding and looked at him.

"Well you have something you want to say to me?"

"Yeah, I understand you went to see a specific special lady the other day."

"Well you know how it is. Some women can't get enough of a good thing he replied. I don't think the special lady minded my being there. At least she didn't get up when I stroked those beautiful thighs under the table and kissed those luscious lips."

Troy's temperature rose and he started to boil.

"I don't know what you're trying to prove or who you think you are fooling, but Tracy is through with you. I can't tell you when or how it happened that we got together, but we are together now and you stay away from her."

"Stay away from her or else what? How quickly you forget who was hitting it and boy was I doing so everywhere and everyplace. She just could not get enough of a brother. All I had to do was touch that babe and she'd begin to get undressed and begging me, sometimes on her hands and knees. I really could make her crawl. I don't think it will be too long before we are at it again because she knows I am the only one that can satisfy her the way she likes it."

Just then, Troy became furious and knocked Richard off the bike with one blow and they went at it. It took several guys to separate them and Dave forced them into his office.

"What the hell do you guys think you are doing? I have a business to run and you are trying to scare my customers away. Both of you have been friends for a long time and you are going to throw all of that away because of some woman."

Troy stated, "Wars have been started because of women."

Dave replied, "Yeah, but look at the fine single women out there. I see them coming through my club daily."

Troy snapped back.

"All the women in the world cannot take the place of that special person. Someone you can truly call your soul mate for life. Someone you want to spend the rest of your life with to make your life complete. I love Tracy to the point that I would do anything in the world for her and this son of a bitch only wants to use her."

He turned to Richard.

"You know what you are Richard. You're a dog and a sex addict and I am just wondering how Jackie would feel if she somehow found out about you and Tracy."

That statement almost started another brawl.

Troy continued, saying "I don't believe you respect women, otherwise you would not be cheating on Jackie."

Richard replied, "I'd kill you before I let you get away with telling Jackie anything." "You know Richard, you are a sick man. I helped you with your little scheme and said nothing to Jackie. I don't have to tell her because the way you are acting, she will figure it out herself. There is however one thing you need to know and that is if you hurt Tracy again, you will regret the day you were born."

"You should be happy for us. If it was not me it would have been someone else."

Richard, looking solemn, started to speak.

"I know you might find this hard to believe but I love Tracy and Jackie equally for different reasons. I've been with Jackie a long time and I'm used to having her around me. She used to be a lot of fun, but everything is so serious with her. She is so busy that we very seldom have sex. When we do make love, she just does not satisfy me or do the things sexually like Tracy will do for me and to me. I need them both to make my life complete. I don't want to leave Jackie right now and I don't want to lose Tracy. I need them both to make my life work."

Troy just shook his head.

"You know, I didn't realize this until now but you are a sick man. I'm glad all I need is Tracy in my life and I'm going to say this once more. Stay the hell away from her, her apartment, her family, and especially her body, otherwise."

Richard interrupted, "Otherwise what? You're going to tell Jackie?"

"I won't have to tell Jackie because she will read about it when they're there dragging your body out of the river"

He slammed the door and left.

Richard said, "Can you believe that he has the nerve to threaten me. Who does he think he is anyway?"

Dave responded, "He's a man in love. You know what? Troy is right. You're sick and you need to get some help and leave those two alone. Now get out of my office."

Troy asked Tracy to pack some evening and fun clothes because he had to go to Aruba on business and he wanted to take her with him. He knew she always wanted to go there. What she did not know is that it was a setup. He had secretly made arrangements for Tracy's sister, her best friend, his best friend and a few other family members including her mom, and his parents to be there. They were to keep it a secret and no one would know where they were going. They arrived in Aruba and it was like being in paradise. Everyone was so happy and friendly and I cannot begin to describe how charming and romantic the island was. We even had a condo on a private beach. I don't know how he arranged that. The bedroom was upstairs and you can see the water splashing onto the sandy beach from the bedroom or the patio. I was so happy.

Troy and I walked on the beach and talked about our future and other plans. It was peaceful and nice to get away from the office and Richard. The next day we went on a shopping spree. Later that evening, Troy asked me to put on one of my sexy outfits because we were going out and he made special arrangements at a restaurant. I chose a red strapless evening dress with a red and white shawl with shoes to match. The dress was soft and showed off my curves. When I stepped out of the bedroom Troy responded as if it were the first time he laid eyes on me. I thought he was going to skip dinner and make love to me right there.

Knowing my love for seafood, he took me to one of the best seafood restaurants on the Island. It was very elegant and we feasted on lobster and champagne. When dinner was done, he asked if I was ready for desert.

"I am so stuffed, I can't eat anything else."

"I would like for you to try a little because I had it made especially just for you."

Just then, the waiter brought over a small dome covered plate. I lifted the cover and found a small box.

"What is this Troy?"

"Open it," he replied. I started to shake and inside was a beautiful pair of diamond earrings. I started to cry when he asked me not to wear them until our wedding day. That day came sooner than I expected. I leaned over and gave him a big kiss. As I was putting the earrings back into the box, Troy grabbed my hand.

"Tracy do you really love me."

"Of course I do, Troy. I have something on my mind. I want you to do something for me.

"What is it? You are beginning to scare me. He walked over to the other side of the table where I was sitting, lifted the flap underneath the earrings, kneeled on one knee, and took out a diamond ring.

"Tracy, I love you more than life itself. Without you I am just an empty shell. I need you to make my life complete. Tracy, I will be the happiest man in the world if you would agree to be my wife. Will you marry me?"

"Troy, I don't know what to say."

"Yes will be nice."

"Troy, of course I will marry you," I said, shaking.

I stopped shaking during his next statement.

"I want you to marry me tonight."

"Marry you tonight?"

"Tracy, I know you always wanted a big wedding. Although I respect your wishes, I can do without the fanfare. I have my reasons for asking you this, but I don't want to go into them now. What I ask is that you marry me in Aruba and then when we return home, we can renew our vowels and have a big wedding. Do you trust me enough to agree to that?"

"Troy, you mean just elope? I don't understand why the rush. I just became engaged. That hasn't set in and you want to get married right now? Besides don't we have to have a witness, blood tests, and a license?"

Tracy do you love me enough to marry me right now with no questions asked?

I looked into his big brown eyes.

"Troy, whatever you say. I feel funny about getting married in this red dress and don't we have to have a license. Also, I just finished eating and I probably look fat."

Just then he pulled out his cell phone and said we are all set. He picked me up twirled me around and brought me into a room where our minister had a license already prepared. I almost fainted when I my sister and best friend came and gave me a hug. The restaurant was attached to a Hotel. They took me to a room where I was transformed in about an hour with a beautiful wedding dress, makeup, hairstyle, and shoes to match.

I found out that the wedding dress was chosen by my sister. We talked about our wedding day and what dress we would like to wear several times.

This was the craziest thing I have ever done in my life. I was still having mixed feelings because I would have liked to have enjoyed my engagement and planned my wedding with my family and friends, but Troy is such a good man it's what he wants. I arrived at a private suite in the hotel and saw Troy's parents, my mom and her new boyfriend and several close friends and relatives. There were about fifteen of us altogether.

My sister held my hand. Everyone started to clap when I entered the room. Troy's brother began singing "Here and Now." I became Mrs. Troy Johnson. It was so wonderful. After we kissed, danced, and had cake, I mentioned to Troy, you were pretty sure of yourself weren't you? What if I had said no? Honey, I'm just happy you said yes.

While we danced, I whispered in Troy's ear.
"Troy, I do appreciate everything you did for me. I just hope when we get back home and renew our vowels you let me make some decisions."

"Do you regret being Mrs. Troy Johnson?"
"No, Troy, of course not. Well, I guess I was thinking with my heart and not my head. I promise you,

when we get back home, I'll do what you want. We will make all future decisions together. I just wanted this to be a surprise."

"Well Mr. Johnson, you accomplished your goal and I love you very much."

I felt much better when my sister talked to me about what a special person Troy was to go through all of this for me and how much he loved me.

"He would do anything for you and just think when you get back; we are going to plan a wedding celebration for you. You aren't pregnant are you?"

"No, I'm not pregnant."

"I guess he just wanted to make a legal woman of you."

"I guess," I replied.

Chapter 6

When we returned from our honeymoon, we began looking for a house. It did not take us long to find the house of our dream. It was a beautiful five bedroom home to fit the family of our future. I felt like I was dreaming. What more could anyone want? While we waited for everything to become final, I went back to my condo to begin packing. Troy had to leave for a weekend to take care of some important business. Everything was falling right into place.

The next day Jackie had called everyone to her house for an important planning meeting. Jackie asked Richard to open a jar for her. While opening the jar, one of the members named Cynthia asked if they heard the good news.

"What good news?"
"Troy and Tracy were married in Aruba a few weeks ago."
"What?"
Richard dropped the jar spilling its contents all over Jackie's outfit.

"I'm sorry honey," he replied. "It just slipped. I'll go to the store and pick up more."

"That's okay, it's not that important. I had better change."

When she left the room, Cynthia became suspicious and began to quiz Richard.

"I thought you and Troy were friends? I didn't mean to be the bearer of bad news. I don't know why he did not invite you and Jackie. He invited others from what I heard."

Without saying a word, he left and headed straight for my condo. He knocked on the door. I was in such a good mood and did not see who was at the door. When I opened the door, all hell broke loose. Richard was furious.

"What are you doing here?" I asked.

He pushed me down and said, "I want to talk with you."

"Get out now," I replied.

He grabbed me off the floor and began to kiss me. I slapped him as hard as I could.

"Richard, you have no business being here. I'm expecting company. You had better leave, now before I call the cops."

He ripped out the phone. I tried to run but he pushed me down again. He turned on the radio.

"Richard, how dare you come in here uninvited?

What do you want?"

"Oh, you hate me that much now? I remember when I was screwing you, you couldn't get enough."

"Richard and I are married now and the past is the past."

"I heard about that phony marriage, but do you really think it makes a difference to me. You forget I'm married too. Now no one will be able to suspect anything when we make love to each other."

"Richard I'm sorry. I love Troy and I'm not going to be cheating on him. I think you had better leave now."

He grabbed a piece of rope out of his pocket. I started to run and scream but could not fight him off. He tied my hands and grabbed me, and threw me on the bed. He snatched my clothes off and began to rape me. I screamed, but the more I screamed, the more violent he became. After raping me, he tied me to the bed and let me stay there half naked while he showered and smoked a cigarette. He stated that he was sick of me crying and acting like a child so he began to beat me with his belt. He then raped me again repeatedly. I cried out for "God" and wondered why no one could hear me screaming. He again began to whip me.

"I'm going to knock some sense into you if it's the last thing I do."

"You belong to me. You'll always belong to me."

I got loose and tried to crawl to the door but he grabbed me back and forced me to crawl to him like a dog. After I calmed down, I realized that he was doing drugs and drinking. This gentle man I once loved changed and become a craved animal.

During the evening, he began to punch me continuously in the face.

"When I'm through with you, you won't be much to look at and Troy won't want you. He tried to throw me off the balcony. Later, he just kicked me repeatedly and laughed. Then he continued to rape me.

While this was going on, Troy had been calling but did not become alarm because he kept getting a busy signal and figured that I was on the phone. He became concerned and called over to Jackie and Richard's house requesting to speak with Richard. He really became concerned when he found out that Richard was not there. He asked his brother Mike and my sister Kathy to stop by the condo to see if everything was okay.

Richard made me get dressed and then forced me into his car driving me to a wooded area, where he raped me again. I thought he was going to kill me so I lied and stated that I would leave Troy and he would be the only man in my life. That made him very happy. I asked if we could go back home now but he said that I would never see that condo again. He took me to a motel instead and claimed that we would stay here for awhile until he could get my old place back.

Back at the condo, my sister Kathy and Troy's brother Mike arrived at the same time to the condo. They called the police when they saw the door was open and there were some signs of a struggle and blood around the room. Mike called Troy back and told him he should get back as soon as possible. He did not want to give him any details on the phone but indicated it does not look good. Troy was only two hours away, but decided to fly back as he would arrive back into Chicago in a half hour. His heart was pounding and he cried when he called my sister Kathy back and she described the scene and what they perceived had taken place. They searched the condo and the neighborhood trying to find me.

Troy made it back in town, and he hailed a cab. The airport was only twenty-five minutes from the house but it appeared that the drive was hours. While they were stopped at a light, Troy happened to see Richard's car. He called the police and assumed from the position of the car that we were in one or two of the apartments. He chose the right room immediately as he heard us talking and me begging Richard to stop. He did not waste anytime as he busted the door down. It broke his heart to see me bloody, beaten with a swollen face and bruises all over my body.

By this time, I was out of my mind. Troy grabbed Richard and they began to fight in the room with me screaming. Richard pulled out a gun and as Troy tried to get the gun away from him it went off. From there all I remember is being in Troy's arms with him crying and begging "God" not to let me die and Richard hollering that it was an accident. I did not mean to hurt her.

I can only imagine how Troy must have felt seeing me in that condition. I so badly wanted to be in his arms, but what if I was disfigured to the point that he could no longer stand to look at me. What would become of me? My heart was breaking and I had to run to him and ask him for forgiveness. I couldn't move. I could only scream. I must have yelled so loud because the man sitting in the chair knocked everything over to reach me and held me as I cried. I looked up and it was Troy. The nurse and the doctor came in and everyone was so happy and it finally dawned on me where I was. They explained to me I had been in a semi-comatose state for a few days. They ran some additional test and it look like I was on my way to recovery from the attack but I could tell something else was wrong.

They waited until I was strong enough and scheduled an appointment with us. When we reached his office the doctor began to explain that I had been infected with HIV. I cried and asked the doctor if I was going to die? Troy also had tears in his eyes and I wondered if he was going to leave me. If he did my life would surely be over. The doctor explained, just because you are diagnosed as HIV Positive, does not mean you will die. The doctor continued to speak, but my thoughts were on him hating that he chose me as his wife.

After we discussed treatments with the doctor, Troy hugged and kissed me. He let me know that he would never leave me, and I knew it was going to be all right.

Troy did not say much to me on the way home or when we arrived at the house. I felt ashamed and alone. He went into the bathroom and it sounded like he was crying, so I left him alone and went upstairs. I felt like ending my life right then and there so he did not have to be bothered with me. I did not know how or what to say to him, so I wrote down my feelings and explained to him that I was sorry for the shame and hurt I put him through. If he wanted to divorce me I would understand. I felt I was no longer fit for him or any other man. I fell asleep before finishing the letter and Troy carried me to the bed and started reading what I wrote down. I must have slept a couple of hours and when I came downstairs he asked me to sit on the couch and then he got on his knees. He held my hands.

"What happened is not your fault. You are my queen we are going to get through this together. We are not going to let Satan steal our dreams and ruin our lives. Once we get through the trial, it will be behind us and we will continue together. If you ever feel down or upset, come to me and with God's help, he will be our strength. He jumped up and was surprised when I told him that I don't know if I want to press charges."

"Of course you are going to press charges. He is going to be charged with attempted murder and put away, I hope for life."

"Troy will you please hear me out, please? "

"Troy, I love you and I do not want to drag this through the court system. It would not be good for business. I could not take the bad publicity. They will drag me down and try to pretend it was consensual because I had been in a relationship with him and he was a married man."

"Baby, I don't care about the business, but I do care about your feelings. I am not happy with your decision, but respect your wishes. I just feel he should have to pay for what he put you through."

"Troy, I really don't think he meant to harm me. I think he lost it because he could not stand us being together."

"That's exactly what I mean. What if we let him go and he tries something again. I find it hard to live that way. "

"Troy lets have faith in God and he will see us through. I am not afraid and I don't want you to be afraid for me. We can get a restraining order and work out something that if he is within three feet of me, we will press charges."

I could see it in his eyes that Troy was still upset and hurt at my decision. That evening we had a quiet dinner and Troy asked my sister to stay with me a little while as he had to go take care of some business.

Troy found out that they had let Richard out on bail and wanted to confront him. He went over to his brother Mike's house first and asked him to come with him for fear that he might hurt Richard and go to jail. He kept telling him that he should be forced to pay for what he did and how he ruined our lives. His brother tried to reason with him and explained if you do kill him and go to jail, who will take care of and look after Tracy. She deserves better than that. He started to cry and his brother let him.

He calmed down and said, "I just want to talk with him."

His brother went with him. When they arrived at the house, Jackie opened the door.

"Where's Richard? We want to talk to him," stated Troy.

"He's not here and I don't know when he will be back."

"Can we come in and wait?"

"No you can't come in here and you have a nerve asking to come in.'

"Richard told me everything."

"He told you everything? Did he tell you how he raped my wife and infected her with HIV?"

"What?"

Jackie almost fainted, but they caught her. She allowed them to come in so they could talk. Troy told Jackie that he was sorry and did not mean to hurt her.

"I better pour both of you a drink because I have something to tell you," said Jackie. "Richard did tell me what happened and he left after I told him I had a feeling he was having an affair with someone, but I never imagined it was Tracy. I have also been having an affair and found out that I had been infected with the virus myself. I should have told Richard long ago, but did not know how. My first affair was with Jennifer and then I slept with your younger brother James."

"James?"

"Yes, we have been sleeping together for about a year now. We really love each other and I am so sorry this happened to you. When I broke up with Jennifer, she became depressed and started using drugs. I tried to comfort her and ended up on drugs myself. I did not know at the time I started sleeping with James that we both were sick."

Troy was so stunned that he dropped the glass. He looked at his other brother, got up and looked at Jackie.

"Jackie, I feel sorry for you and Richard both. You are a screwed up pair and you deserve each other. You just ruined not only your lives but mine and Tracy's life with your selfishness. When will all this deceit end? You let your desires get the best of you."

They left. Troy was doing the driving. When he saw Richard's car at the bar, his blood pressure began to rise. He almost drove into the place trying to park the car. His brother tried to tell him to take it slow but he rushed into the bar and started looking around. He saw Richard at the bar drinking. Troy immediately pulled him off the bar stool and started beating him. He was enraged as he yelled you dirty dog I trusted you and you raped my wife. A half-drunk Richard tried to fight back but it took six men to pull Troy from him. The men kept them separated. Troy's brother kept telling him to think about Tracy and think about what Richard is going to have to face when he gets home. Troy began to settle down.

"Why did you have to treat her like that? You told me you loved her. I would hate to see what you do to someone you hate," Troy told him, crying.

"I'm so sorry, man. I didn't mean to hurt her."

"Well, you did more than just hurt her. You scarred her for life and I hope she lives long enough to put not only your sorry ass, but Jackie's behind bars."

"You leave Jackie out of this. I'm the only one to blame."

"I wish I could start all over and take everything back. I feel like my world is ending."

Jackie told him about the affair and now he lost Tracy too.

"I would rather lose my arms than to put either of you through that pain. I took my frustration and anger out on the woman I really loved because I thought she had betrayed me when I should have taken it out on Jackie, but how could I because I was doing the same thing myself. I am sorry and I ask that you both please forgive me. I felt if I could make love to her one more time, she would come back to me, but she kept refusing saying that she only wanted you and no one else to touch her. I was wrong. All I can do is ask for both of you to forgive me. If it takes the rest of my life, I will make it up to you both. I wish I could take both of your pain away."

"I am going to pray for you," said Troy. He and his brother left.

I decided not to press charges against Richard. It took a tragic incident like this to break up Richard and Jackie who finally divorced. Jackie became involved with an Aids Research organization and is doing well. I began treatment and am on my way to recovering from the ordeal. I still have nightmares about the entire incident, but when I awake Troy is always by my side. Troy and I went on to build a successful business and we have two wonderful, healthy children. We never heard from Richard again..

QUICK ORDER FORM
What My Heart Desires
List price $9.95
Website: www.annsbusinesssolutions.com
www.lastingimpressionbooks.com
Email: lastingimpressionbooks@yahoo.com
Telephone Number: 1-877-855-8989 Ext 102
Shipping by air-U.S. Local-Please add $1.00 for each book.
Non-Local: Please add $2.00 for the first book, and $1.00 for each additional book (estimate).
For speaking engagements, seminars, or interviews, call, email, or mail request to the addresses listed below.

16845 N. 29th Ave #616, Phoenix AZ 85053
Story by Ann M. Hampton, (c)
Copyright Protected

What My Heart Desires
Publisher Information
Vaughanworks Publishing
Website: www.vaughanworks.com
Email: vaughanworks@sbcglobal.net
Telephone Number: 1-877-VAWORKS (829-6757) toll
free.
Vaughanworks Mailing Address
P.O. Box 44224
West Allis, WI 53214 USA